Daniel Misses Someone

Adapted by Alexandra Cassel Schwartz
Based on the screenplay written by Mary Jacobson
Poses and layouts by Jason Fruchter

Simon Spotlight
New York London Toronto Sydney New Delhi

SIMON SPOTLIGHT

An imprint of Simon & Schuster Children's Publishing Division
1230 Avenue of the Americas, New York, New York 10020
This Simon Spotlight edition December 2021
© 2021 The Fred Rogers Company. All Rights Reserved.
All rights reserved, including the right of reproduction in whole or in part in any form.
SIMON SPOTLIGHT and colophon are registered trademarks of Simon & Schuster, Inc.
For information about special discounts for bulk purchases, please contact Simon & Schuster
Special Sales at 1-866-506-1949 or business@simonandschuster.com.
Manufactured in the United States of America 1021 LAK
10 9 8 7 6 5 4 3 2 1
ISBN 978-1-6659-0007-2
ISBN 978-1-6659-0008-9 (ebook)

It was a beautiful day in the neighborhood, and Daniel's Grandpere was visiting! Grandpere lived far away from the neighborhood, so seeing him was a special treat for Daniel.

Daniel loved spending time with Grandpere. They liked to bake together, read stories together, and play pretend together too! "Can you guess what we're pretending to be?" asked Daniel.

Soon, it was time for Grandpere to leave and go back home. "But you live so far away," Daniel said. "I'll miss you." Grandpere would miss Daniel too. He sang,

♪ ♫ *"When I miss you, there are things I can do!"* ♪ ♪

"Like what?" Daniel asked.

Grandpere pulled out a photo of Daniel and himself. "Sometimes when I miss you, I look at a picture of us together. It helps me feel better," Grandpere explained.

He gave a copy of the photo to Daniel so that he could look at it whenever he missed Grandpere too.

Ding, ding! Trolley was waiting outside. Grandpere gave Daniel a great big tiger hug. "Even when we're apart, I'll think of you in my heart," he said.

DING!
DING!

Grandpere climbed aboard Trolley, buckled up, and waved goodbye.

"Bye," Daniel said sadly as he watched Trolley disappear down the street.

Daniel already missed Grandpere. He looked at the photo he received and gave it a little hug. "It's hard when we miss the people we love," Mom Tiger said.

♪ ♫ *"When I miss you, there are things I can do!"* *♪ ♩*

Daniel thought about something he could do. "When I can't give a hug to Grandpere, maybe I can give Tigey a hug instead?" Daniel tried giving Tigey a hug, and that did make him feel a little better.

Then Daniel decided to draw a picture. "I'll draw Grandpere and me pretending to sail on his boat," Daniel said. "Ahoy, matey!"

Daniel giggled, thinking about all the fun things he's done with Grandpere.

"I want to send my drawing to Grandpere in the mail," Daniel said. "That way, when Grandpere misses me, he can look at the drawing and feel happy too!"

Mom Tiger thought that was a wonderful idea.

"Hey! Do you want to make believe with me?" Daniel asked. "Let's make believe all kinds of ways Grandpere and I can send love to each other."

Send a hug and a kiss
to the person you miss.
Send a hug and a kiss
to the person you miss.
I'll write a note in a
paper airplane
and throw it high
in the sky.

And when it reaches
your boat,
I hope you like my sweet,
sweet note.

I'll write a message in a bottle
and send it across the sea.
And when it reaches
your shore,
I hope you know I miss
you more.

Getting a letter from you
always makes my day.
Send a hug and a kiss
to the person you miss.
Send a hug and a kiss
to the person you miss.
Send love!

Soon, Prince Wednesday came over to play. They pretended to be baseball players.

"Your big brother is the best baseball player! Maybe we can go play with him," Daniel said.

"No, we can't," Prince Wednesday said. He sat down and sighed. "Prince Tuesday moved away to college."

"What's college?" Daniel asked.

"College is school, but for older kids," Prince Wednesday explained. "Prince Tuesday learns there and lives there too. I really miss him."

Prince Wednesday missed his big brother, just like Daniel missed his Grandpere. Daniel said,

♪ ♫ *"When I miss you, there are things I can do."* ♪ ♫

"What can I do?" Prince Wednesday asked.

"You can make Prince Tuesday something, like how I made a drawing for Grandpere!" Daniel said.

"Rrroyally good idea," Prince Wednesday said. "Maybe we can send them boxes of their favorite things!"

Mom Tiger gave the boys empty boxes to use. They decorated the outside with crayon drawings and heart stickers. Then they filled them with special treats, like drawings and pumpkin muffins.

Prince Wednesday even found a friendship rock to put inside his box. "When Prince Tuesday sees this rock, he'll think of me!" he said.

Daniel and Prince Wednesday gave their boxes to Mr. McFeely to send in the mail.

"I have a delivery for you, Prince Wednesday!" Mr. McFeely said. It was a postcard from Prince Tuesday!

Mom Tiger read the postcard out loud. It said, "Dear Prince Wednesday, I miss you. I'll be coming home to visit you soon. Say 'hi' to Little D for me!" Daniel was so happy that Prince Tuesday was thinking of him, too!

"I miss Grandpere and Prince Tuesday, but there are things I can do until I see them again," Daniel said. "What can YOU do when you miss someone? Ugga Mugga!"